Erogenous Zones in Male and Female Body

A Comprehensive Exploration Guide to Arousal Zones in the Male and Female Body for Heightened Sexuality, and Improved Intimacy and How to Stimulate Them

Wendy Chad

Erogenous Zones in Male and Female Body

© 2024 by Wendy Chad

All rights reserved. No part of this book may be reproduced, stored in a retrieval system, or transmitted, in any form or by any means, electronic, mechanical, photocopying, recording, or otherwise, without prior written permission from the author, except in the case of brief quotations embodied in critical articles and reviews.

The information provided in this book is intended for general informational purposes only, and the author and publisher make no guarantees regarding its accuracy, completeness, or suitability for specific purposes. Readers are advised to seek professional advice tailored to their individual circumstances and should not rely solely on the content presented herein. The book does not provide legal, financial, medical, or professional advice, and the author and publisher disclaim any liability for errors, omissions, or consequences resulting from the use of the information. References to external websites, products, or services are included for reader convenience and do not constitute endorsements. The author's views are personal and not representative of any official policy or position, and all trademarks or copyrights mentioned are the property of their respective owners. This disclaimer is subject to change, and readers are encouraged to review it periodically for updates.

First Edition: 2024

Printed in United States of America

Distributed by Amazon.com, Inc.

Wendy Chad

Dedication

To all seekers of pleasure, intimacy, and connection, may this guide serve as a compass on your journey of exploration and discovery. May you embrace the richness of erogenous zones in the male and female body, unlocking new realms of pleasure and deepening your bonds of intimacy. With gratitude for your curiosity and courage, may you find joy, fulfillment, and profound connection in every moment of exploration.

Erogenous Zones in Male and Female Body

Table of Contents

Dedication _____ *3*

Table of Contents _____ *4*

Chapter 1 _____ *9*

   Introduction _____ **9**

      Overview of the Book and Its Purpose _____ 10

      Importance of Understanding Erogenous Zones for Heightened Sexuality and Improved Intimacy _____ 11

Chapter 2 _____ *13*

   The Science of Erogenous Zones _____ **13**

      Erogenous Zones and How They Work _____ 13

      Neurology and Physiology behind Arousal and Pleasure _ 15

Chapter 3 _____ *19*

   Male Erogenous Zones _____ **19**

      Scrotum and Testicles _____ 19

      Penis (Head, Shaft, Frenulum) _____ 21

Perineum _____22

Inner Thighs and Groin Area _____22

Chest, Nipples, and Navel _____23

Collarbone, Neck, and Ear _____23

Embracing the Full Body Experience _____24

Chapter 4 _____27

Female Erogenous Zones _____27

Breasts and Nipples _____28

Neck, Collarbone, and Chest _____29

Inner Thighs, Knees, and Calves _____29

Clitoris (Head, Hood, and Shaft) _____30

Labia Majora and Labia Minora _____31

Vulva and Vaginal Entrance _____31

Anus and Perianal Area _____32

Abdomen and Navel _____33

Embracing the Full Body Experience _____33

Chapter 5 _____35

Stimulation Techniques _____35

General Tips for Effective Stimulation _____35

Techniques Specific to Male Erogenous Zones _____37

Techniques Specific to Female Erogenous Zones _____38

Oral and Manual Exploration Techniques _____40

Erogenous Zones in Male and Female Body

Utilizing Sex Toys and Props for Erogenous Zone Stimulation _____ 41

Chapter 6 _____ 43

Communication and Consent _____ 43

The Importance of Clear Communication and Consent in Sexual Experiences _____ 43

Asking for and Giving Feedback on Stimulation _____ 44

Recognizing Nonverbal Cues and Reactions _____ 45

Creating an Environment of Trust and Respect _____ 47

Chapter 7 _____ 49

Integrating Erogenous Zones into Sexual Experiences ___ 49

Combining Stimulation of Different Zones for Heightened Pleasure _____ 50

Incorporating Sensory Elements _____ 51

Exploring Role-Play and Fantasies _____ 52

Chapter 8 _____ 55

Enhancing Intimacy through Erogenous Zone Stimulation _____ 55

Building Trust and Emotional Connection through Shared Arousal _____ 56

Using Erogenous Zone Stimulation in Foreplay and Romance _____ 57

Wendy Chad

Engaging in Non-Penetrative Sexual Activities that Focus on Erogenous Zones ____59

Chapter 9 ____61

Personalization and Variation ____61

Catering to Individual Preferences and Desires ____61

Discovering New Erogenous Zones and Arousal Patterns over Time ____63

Embracing Fluidity in Arousal and Pleasure Responses __64

Chapter 10 ____67

Beyond the Basics: Advanced Topics and Techniques __67

Tantric and Energetic Approaches to Erogenous Zone Stimulation ____68

BDSM Practices and Erogenous Zone Play ____69

Group Play and Partner Swapping Involving Erogenous Zone Stimulation ____71

Chapter 11 ____75

Enhancing Your Sexual Experience with Erogenous Zone Stimulation ____75

Putting It All Together: Incorporating Knowledge into Your Sexual Experiences ____76

Finding New Ways to Explore and Enjoy Erogenous Zones 77

Erogenous Zones in Male and Female Body

The Power of Curiosity and Open-Mindedness in Enhancing Your Sexuality_____78

_Conclusion _____81_

A Journey of Discovery _____81

Empowerment through Knowledge_____82

Embracing Diversity and Fluidity _____82

Continued Growth and Exploration _____83

Closing Thoughts _____83

Wendy Chad

Chapter 1

Introduction

Welcome to "Erogenous Zones in Male and Female Body: A Comprehensive Exploration Guide to Arousal Zones in the Male and Female Body for Heightened Sexuality, and Improved Intimacy and How to Stimulate Them". In this book, we embark on an enlightening journey to explore the intricacies of erogenous zones in both male and female bodies. From the tantalizing touch points that ignite passion to the pathways of pleasure that deepen intimacy, we delve into the essential knowledge and techniques for unlocking heightened sexuality and enhancing intimacy through the stimulation of erogenous zones.

Erogenous Zones in Male and Female Body

Overview of the Book and Its Purpose

This book is a comprehensive guide designed to provide readers with a deeper understanding of erogenous zones in both male and female bodies. Through a detailed exploration of anatomy, physiology, and sexual response, we aim to equip readers with the knowledge and techniques needed to enhance their sexual experiences and deepen their intimacy with their partners.

Throughout the chapters, we will examine various erogenous zones in the male and female bodies, including but not limited to the obvious areas such as the genitals, as well as lesser-known areas that can be equally as arousing. We will discuss the unique characteristics of each erogenous zone, explore different methods of stimulation, and provide practical tips and techniques for maximizing pleasure and satisfaction.

Wendy Chad

Importance of Understanding Erogenous Zones for Heightened Sexuality and Improved Intimacy

Understanding erogenous zones is essential for unlocking heightened sexuality and improving intimacy in relationships. Erogenous zones are areas of the body that are particularly sensitive to sexual stimulation and can elicit pleasurable sensations when touched, kissed, or caressed. By familiarizing ourselves with these zones and learning how to stimulate them effectively, we can enhance our sexual experiences and deepen our connection with our partners.

Moreover, the exploration of erogenous zones fosters a deeper understanding of our own bodies and desires. It encourages us to communicate openly with our partners about our preferences and boundaries, creating a safe and supportive environment for sexual

Erogenous Zones in Male and Female Body

exploration and experimentation. As a result, understanding erogenous zones can lead to increased sexual satisfaction, heightened arousal, and improved intimacy in our relationships.

In conclusion, this book is intended to serve as a comprehensive resource for anyone interested in unlocking the secrets of erogenous zones and harnessing their power for heightened sexuality and improved intimacy. Whether you're a novice explorer or a seasoned aficionado, may the knowledge and techniques presented in these pages inspire you to embark on a journey of discovery and pleasure unlike any other.

Chapter 2

The Science of Erogenous Zones

Erogenous zones are the key to unlocking heightened arousal, pleasure, and intimacy in sexual encounters. In this chapter, we delve into the intricate science behind erogenous zones, exploring what they are, how they work, and the neurology and physiology that underpin arousal and pleasure.

Erogenous Zones and How They Work

Erogenous zones are areas of the body that are particularly sensitive to sexual stimulation and can elicit pleasurable sensations when touched, kissed, or caressed. These zones vary from person to person and can include both external and internal areas of the

Erogenous Zones in Male and Female Body

body. While some erogenous zones are well-known, such as the genitals, others may be less obvious, such as the neck, ears, or inner thighs.

The sensitivity of erogenous zones is due to a high concentration of nerve endings, which transmit signals to the brain when stimulated. These nerve endings are connected to the brain's pleasure centers, triggering the release of neurotransmitters such as dopamine and endorphins, which are associated with feelings of pleasure and reward.

Erogenous zones can also be influenced by psychological factors such as anticipation, desire, and emotional connection. When we engage in sexual activity with a partner whom we trust and feel emotionally connected to, the sensations experienced in erogenous zones can be heightened, leading to more intense pleasure and arousal.

Neurology and Physiology behind Arousal and Pleasure

The neurology and physiology behind arousal and pleasure are complex and multifaceted, involving a combination of neural pathways, hormones, and psychological factors.

When a person becomes sexually aroused, the brain sends signals to the autonomic nervous system, which controls involuntary bodily functions such as heart rate, blood pressure, and respiration. This triggers a cascade of physiological responses, including increased blood flow to the genitals, lubrication in the vagina, and erection of the penis.

The release of neurotransmitters such as dopamine, serotonin, and oxytocin further enhances feelings of

Erogenous Zones in Male and Female Body

pleasure and arousal. Dopamine, in particular, is associated with the brain's reward system and is released in response to pleasurable stimuli, reinforcing the desire for sexual activity.

Oxytocin, often referred to as the "love hormone," plays a key role in bonding and intimacy. It is released during sexual activity and promotes feelings of trust, connection, and emotional closeness between partners.

Additionally, the release of endorphins during sexual activity can act as natural pain relievers, reducing discomfort and enhancing feelings of pleasure.

In conclusion, the science of erogenous zones offers valuable insights into the mechanisms of arousal and pleasure in sexual encounters. By understanding the neurology and physiology behind erogenous zones,

Wendy Chad

we can better appreciate the complexities of sexual response and explore ways to enhance arousal and pleasure in our own experiences.

Erogenous Zones in Male and Female Body

Chapter 3

Male Erogenous Zones

Understanding the erogenous zones of the male body is a crucial aspect of exploring and enhancing sexual pleasure and intimacy. In this chapter, we delve into the intricate landscapes of male erogenous zones, exploring their anatomy, sensitivity, and the various techniques to stimulate them for heightened arousal and intimacy.

Scrotum and Testicles

The scrotum and testicles are highly sensitive areas rich in nerve endings, making them prime erogenous zones for men. The scrotum, a sac of skin containing the testicles, is particularly sensitive to touch and

Erogenous Zones in Male and Female Body

temperature variations. Gentle stroking, caressing, and light tugging of the scrotum can elicit intense sensations of pleasure. Experiment with different pressures and textures to find what feels best for you or your partner.

When it comes to the testicles themselves, they are incredibly sensitive to both pleasure and pain. Approach them with care and communicate openly with your partner about their preferences. Lightly massaging the testicles or gently cupping them can be incredibly arousing for many men. Some may enjoy the sensation of having their testicles lightly sucked or licked, while others may prefer more indirect stimulation. Remember, individual preferences vary, so always prioritize communication and consent.

Wendy Chad

Penis (Head, Shaft, Frenulum)

The penis is undoubtedly one of the most well-known erogenous zones in the male body. Consisting of the head (glans), shaft, and frenulum (the sensitive strip of skin on the underside of the penis), each area offers unique sensations when stimulated.

The glans, densely packed with nerve endings, is particularly sensitive to touch, making it a focal point for arousal. Experiment with different strokes, pressures, and techniques, such as gentle licking, sucking, or kissing, to discover what brings the most pleasure.

The shaft of the penis is also highly sensitive, albeit to a lesser degree than the glans. Running your hands or tongue along the shaft, varying pressure and speed, can heighten arousal and build anticipation.

Erogenous Zones in Male and Female Body

The frenulum, often referred to as the male equivalent of the clitoris due to its sensitivity, is a hotspot for pleasure. Gentle stimulation of the frenulum, such as light touches or flicks with the tongue, can produce intense sensations of pleasure and arousal.

Perineum

The perineum, located between the anus and the scrotum, is a lesser-known but highly erogenous zone in men. Stimulating the perineum can indirectly activate the prostate gland, adding a new dimension to sexual pleasure. Light pressure or circular motions with fingers or tongue can awaken sensations of pleasure and arousal.

Inner Thighs and Groin Area

The inner thighs and groin area are often overlooked but can be incredibly sensitive erogenous zones for men. Lightly tracing your fingers or lips along the inner thighs, moving closer to the groin with teasing touches, can build anticipation and arousal. Experiment with varying pressure and proximity to the genitals to gauge your partner's response.

Chest, Nipples, and Navel

While not exclusive to women, the chest, nipples, and navel are also erogenous zones for many men. Gentle caresses, kisses, or nibbles on the chest and nipples can elicit pleasurable sensations and enhance arousal. Pay attention to your partner's reactions and adjust your touch accordingly to maximize pleasure.

Collarbone, Neck, and Ear

The collarbone, neck, and ear are highly sensitive areas rich in nerve endings, making them ideal for sensual stimulation. Soft kisses, nibbles, or gentle

Erogenous Zones in Male and Female Body

breaths along the collarbone and neck can send shivers down the spine and heighten arousal. Whispering sweet nothings or lightly blowing air into the ear can also be incredibly arousing for many men.

Embracing the Full Body Experience

While exploring erogenous zones is undeniably exciting, it's essential to remember that sexual pleasure extends beyond individual body parts. Embracing the full-body experience involves engaging all the senses and focusing on connection and intimacy.

Communication, trust, and mutual exploration are key components of enhancing sexual pleasure and intimacy. Take the time to communicate openly with your partner about desires, boundaries, and preferences. Experiment with different techniques, listen to your partner's feedback, and adjust

Wendy Chad

accordingly to create a deeply satisfying and intimate experience for both of you.

In conclusion, understanding and exploring male erogenous zones can open up new avenues of pleasure and intimacy in your sexual experiences. From the scrotum and testicles to the chest and neck, each area offers unique sensations waiting to be discovered. Embrace the journey of exploration with curiosity, communication, and a sense of adventure, and watch as your sexual encounters reach new heights of pleasure and connection.

Erogenous Zones in Male and Female Body

Chapter 4

Female Erogenous Zones

Ever wondered what makes a woman tremble with pleasure and gasp for air during intimate moments? The answer lies in understanding her erogenous zones. While the conventional wisdom associates female pleasure primarily with the genitals, there's a whole universe of sensitive spots that can ignite intense feelings of desire and lust.

Exploring the erogenous zones of the female body is a journey of discovery and intimacy. In this chapter, we delve into the intricacies of female erogenous zones, from the well-known to the often-overlooked, exploring

Erogenous Zones in Male and Female Body

their anatomy, sensitivity, and the various techniques to stimulate them for heightened arousal and intimacy.

Breasts and Nipples

The breasts and nipples are perhaps the most universally recognized erogenous zones in the female body. The breasts, comprised of fatty tissue and mammary glands, are sensitive to touch and pressure. Gently caressing, massaging, or cupping the breasts can evoke pleasurable sensations and build arousal. Experiment with different strokes, pressures, and techniques to discover what feels best for you or your partner.

The nipples, located at the center of each breast, are particularly sensitive to touch and temperature variations. Lightly tracing circles around the nipples, kissing, licking, or gently nibbling on them can elicit intense sensations of pleasure and arousal. Pay attention to your partner's responses and adjust your touch accordingly to maximize pleasure.

Neck, Collarbone, and Chest

The neck, collarbone, and chest are rich in nerve endings, making them prime erogenous zones for many women. Soft kisses, nibbles, or gentle caresses along the neck and collarbone can send shivers down the spine and heighten arousal. Lightly running your fingers or tongue along the chest can also evoke pleasurable sensations and build anticipation.

Inner Thighs, Knees, and Calves

The inner thighs, knees, and calves are often overlooked but can be highly sensitive erogenous zones for women. Lightly tracing your fingers or lips along the inner thighs, moving closer to the knees with teasing touches, can build anticipation and arousal.

Erogenous Zones in Male and Female Body

Experiment with varying pressure and proximity to the genitals to gauge your partner's response.

Clitoris (Head, Hood, and Shaft)

The clitoris is a powerhouse of pleasure, with thousands of nerve endings dedicated solely to sensation. Understanding the anatomy of the clitoris is crucial for maximizing pleasure and arousal.

The clitoral head, located at the top of the vulva, is the most sensitive part of the clitoris. Gentle stimulation with fingers, tongue, or a vibrator can elicit intense sensations of pleasure. The clitoral hood, a fold of skin that covers the clitoral head, protects it from overstimulation. Lightly retracting the clitoral hood or applying gentle pressure around the clitoral shaft can enhance arousal.

The clitoral shaft, extending from the clitoral head down towards the vaginal opening, is also highly sensitive to stimulation. Experiment with different strokes, pressures, and techniques to discover what brings the most pleasure for you or your partner.

Labia Majora and Labia Minora

The labia majora and labia minora are the outer and inner folds of skin surrounding the vaginal opening, respectively. Both areas are rich in nerve endings and sensitive to touch. Gently stroking or caressing the labia with fingers or tongue can evoke pleasurable sensations and build arousal. Experiment with different pressures and techniques to discover what feels best.

Erogenous Zones in Male and Female Body

Vulva and Vaginal Entrance

The vulva, comprising the external female genitalia, is a complex network of erogenous zones. The clitoris, labia, and vaginal entrance all contribute to sensations of pleasure and arousal. Experiment with different touches, pressures, and techniques to explore the full range of sensations available.

The vaginal entrance, located just below the clitoris, is also highly sensitive to stimulation. Gentle penetration with fingers or a sex toy, accompanied by plenty of lubrication and communication, can enhance arousal and pleasure.

Anus and Perianal Area

The anus and perianal area are often overlooked but can be highly sensitive erogenous zones for many women. Lightly massaging or caressing the area around the anus with fingers or tongue can evoke pleasurable sensations and build anticipation. Remember to communicate openly with your partner about desires, boundaries, and preferences when exploring this area.

Abdomen and Navel

The abdomen and navel are lesser-known but can be surprisingly sensitive erogenous zones for some women. Gentle touches, kisses, or nibbles along the abdomen and around the navel can evoke pleasurable sensations and heighten arousal. Experiment with different pressures and techniques to discover what feels best for you or your partner.

Embracing the Full Body Experience

Embracing the full-body experience involves engaging all the senses and focusing on connection and

Erogenous Zones in Male and Female Body

intimacy. Communication, trust, and mutual exploration are key components of enhancing sexual pleasure and intimacy. Take the time to communicate openly with your partner about desires, boundaries, and preferences. Experiment with different techniques, listen to your partner's feedback, and adjust accordingly to create a deeply satisfying and intimate experience for both of you.

In conclusion, understanding and exploring female erogenous zones can open up new avenues of pleasure and intimacy in your sexual experiences. From the breasts and nipples to the clitoris and vaginal entrance, each area offers unique sensations waiting to be discovered. Embrace the journey of exploration with curiosity, communication, and a sense of adventure, and watch as your sexual encounters reach new heights of pleasure and connection.

Chapter 5

Stimulation Techniques

Mastering the art of stimulation is essential for unlocking the full potential of erogenous zones and enhancing sexual pleasure and intimacy. In this chapter, we explore a variety of techniques tailored to both male and female erogenous zones, along with general tips for effective stimulation and the use of sex toys and props to enhance the experience.

General Tips for Effective Stimulation

Pace: The pace of stimulation can make or break the experience. Start slow to build anticipation and gradually increase intensity as arousal heightens. Pay

Erogenous Zones in Male and Female Body

close attention to your partner's cues to gauge the optimal pace.

Pressure: Experiment with different levels of pressure to discover what feels best. Some may prefer gentle, feather-light touches, while others crave firmer pressure. Communication is key to understanding preferences.

Variation: Keep stimulation varied to prevent monotony and maintain arousal. Alternate between light touches, firm strokes, and teasing caresses to keep the senses heightened and the anticipation alive.

Exploration: Don't limit yourself to familiar erogenous zones. Explore lesser-known areas of the body, such as the inner thighs, neck, ears, and lower back. You may stumble upon new sources of pleasure waiting to be awakened.

Wendy Chad

Communication: Above all, communicate openly with your partner. Share desires, preferences, and boundaries to ensure a mutually satisfying experience. Encourage feedback and adjust your approach accordingly.

Techniques Specific to Male Erogenous Zones

Penis Massage: Begin with gentle strokes along the shaft using varying pressure. Experiment with different techniques, such as circular motions, light tapping, and long, slow glides. Pay special attention to the sensitive head and frenulum for heightened sensation.

Testicle Manipulation: Handle the testicles with care, applying gentle pressure and light massaging motions. Experiment with cupping, rolling, and tugging motions, taking care to avoid excessive force. Incorporate

Erogenous Zones in Male and Female Body

temperature play by alternating between warm and cool sensations.

Perineum Stimulation: The perineum, located between the scrotum and anus, is highly sensitive to touch. Apply firm pressure and circular motions to this area, or experiment with gentle tapping and kneading for added pleasure.

Techniques Specific to Female Erogenous Zones

Breast and Nipple Stimulation: Begin by tracing circles around the areola with your fingertips, gradually increasing pressure. Experiment with sucking, licking, and gentle nibbling of the nipples to enhance arousal. Pay attention to your partner's response and adjust accordingly.

Clitoral Massage: Start with gentle caresses around the clitoral hood, gradually increasing pressure and speed as arousal builds. Experiment with circular motions, light tapping, and rhythmic strokes to stimulate the entire clitoral area. Consider incorporating lubrication for added comfort and sensation.

Vulva and Vaginal Area Touch: Explore the entire vulva with your fingers, tracing the outer lips, inner labia, and clitoral hood. Experiment with different textures and sensations, such as smooth strokes, gentle kneading, and light tapping. Pay attention to the G-spot, located on the front wall of the vagina, and experiment with various angles and pressures to stimulate it effectively.

Anal Play: Approach anal stimulation with care and respect for your partner's boundaries. Begin with gentle external caresses around the anal opening, gradually progressing to light penetration with a lubricated finger or small anal toy. Communication and consent are essential when exploring this sensitive area.

Oral and Manual Exploration Techniques

Oral Stimulation: Use your tongue, lips, and mouth to explore your partner's erogenous zones with precision and passion. Experiment with different techniques, such as licking, sucking, and gentle nibbling, to elicit pleasurable responses. Pay attention to rhythm and pressure, and be responsive to your partner's cues.

Manual Stimulation: Hands can be incredibly versatile tools for arousal and pleasure. Experiment with different strokes, pressures, and movements to discover what feels best for your partner. Incorporate lubrication for smoother, more pleasurable sensations.

Wendy Chad

Utilizing Sex Toys and Props for Erogenous Zone Stimulation

Vibrators: Vibrators can be invaluable tools for targeting specific erogenous zones with precision and intensity. Experiment with different types of vibrators, such as bullet vibrators, wand massagers, and rabbit vibrators, to discover what works best for you and your partner.

Dildos and Anal Toys: Dildos and anal toys can add variety and excitement to stimulation techniques. Choose toys of appropriate size and shape, and always use plenty of lubrication to ensure comfort and pleasure. Communicate openly with your partner about desires and boundaries when introducing toys into play.

Erogenous Zones in Male and Female Body

Sensory Props: Incorporate sensory props, such as silk scarves, feathers, and blindfolds, to enhance arousal and heighten anticipation. Experiment with temperature play by incorporating ice cubes or warm massage oils into your playtime. Be creative and open-minded in exploring new sensations and experiences together.

In mastering stimulation techniques, remember that the journey is as important as the destination. Approach each touch, each caress, and each exploration with mindfulness, curiosity, and a spirit of adventure. Through open communication, mutual respect, and a willingness to explore, you and your partner can unlock new realms of pleasure and intimacy, enriching your connection in profound and meaningful ways.

Chapter 6

Communication and Consent

Clear communication and enthusiastic consent serve as the guiding stars, illuminating the path to mutual pleasure and profound connection. In this chapter, we explore the pivotal role of communication and consent in sexual experiences, emphasizing the importance of asking for and giving feedback, recognizing nonverbal cues and reactions, and fostering an environment of trust and respect.

The Importance of Clear Communication and Consent in Sexual Experiences

Communication and consent form the cornerstone of healthy, fulfilling sexual encounters. By openly discussing desires, boundaries, and expectations, partners can ensure that their interactions are mutually enjoyable and respectful. Clear communication allows individuals to express their needs and preferences, paving the way for greater intimacy and satisfaction.

Consent, too, is paramount. It is not merely the absence of a "no" but the enthusiastic and ongoing affirmation of a "yes." Consent is freely given, reversible, informed, enthusiastic, and specific. It is a continuous process that requires active participation and mutual respect from all parties involved.

Asking for and Giving Feedback on Stimulation

Effective communication during sexual stimulation involves both asking for and giving feedback. Partners should feel empowered to express what feels pleasurable and what doesn't, allowing for adjustments and refinements to enhance the experience.

When asking for feedback, approach the conversation with sensitivity and openness. Encourage your partner to share their thoughts and feelings without fear of judgment or reprisal. Listen attentively, and be receptive to their cues and signals.

Similarly, when giving feedback, strive to be constructive and encouraging. Express appreciation for what feels good, while gently offering guidance on areas that could be improved. Remember that feedback is a two-way street, and fostering a culture of open communication benefits both partners.

Erogenous Zones in Male and Female Body

Recognizing Nonverbal Cues and Reactions

In addition to verbal communication, paying attention to nonverbal cues and reactions is essential for gauging your partner's enjoyment and comfort level. Nonverbal communication can manifest in subtle gestures, facial expressions, and body language, providing valuable insights into your partner's state of arousal and pleasure.

Be attuned to your partner's breathing patterns, moans, and movements, which can offer clues about what feels pleasurable and what may be uncomfortable. Take cues from their body language, such as relaxed muscles, flushed skin, and increased responsiveness, as indicators of arousal and enjoyment.

However, it's important to note that nonverbal cues are not always straightforward and can vary from person to person. Establishing clear communication beforehand and regularly checking in with your partner ensures that you're both on the same page and able to navigate the nuances of nonverbal communication effectively.

Creating an Environment of Trust and Respect

Above all, creating an environment of trust and respect is essential for fostering open communication and enthusiastic consent. Cultivate a safe space where both partners feel valued, heard, and supported in expressing their desires and boundaries.

Respect your partner's autonomy and agency, and never pressure or coerce them into any sexual activity they're not comfortable with. Prioritize mutual pleasure and well-being, and approach each interaction with empathy, kindness, and understanding.

Erogenous Zones in Male and Female Body

By prioritizing clear communication, enthusiastic consent, and mutual respect, partners can cultivate deeper intimacy and connection in their sexual experiences. Embrace vulnerability, curiosity, and a willingness to learn and grow together, and let communication and consent be the guiding stars that lead you on a journey of exploration and pleasure.

Chapter 7

Integrating Erogenous Zones into Sexual Experiences

In the harmony of sexual pleasure, the integration of erogenous zones serves as the crescendo, orchestrating a harmonious blend of sensation and connection. In this chapter, we explore the art of combining stimulation from different zones for heightened pleasure, incorporating sensory elements to tantalize the senses, and delving into the realms of role-play and fantasy to ignite passion and creativity.

Erogenous Zones in Male and Female Body

Combining Stimulation of Different Zones for Heightened Pleasure

The human body is a mosaic of pleasure, with erogenous zones waiting to be explored and savored. By combining stimulation from multiple zones, partners can create a symphony of sensation that reverberates throughout the body, intensifying pleasure and deepening intimacy.

Experiment with integrating stimulation from both primary and secondary erogenous zones. For example, while focusing on genital stimulation, incorporate touches to other sensitive areas such as the neck, ears, and inner thighs. Alternate between different zones to maintain arousal and prolong the pleasure.

Consider the interconnectedness of erogenous zones and how stimulation in one area can enhance sensitivity and pleasure in others. Explore the erogenous zones as interconnected pathways to pleasure, allowing sensations to ebb and flow between them like a dance of desire.

Incorporating Sensory Elements

Sensory elements play a vital role in heightening arousal and enriching sexual experiences. By engaging all the senses—touch, taste, smell, sound, and temperature—partners can create a multi-dimensional tapestry of sensation that transcends the physical realm.

Experiment with incorporating various textures, such as silk scarves, feather ticklers, or textured massage oils, to tantalize the sense of touch. Explore the interplay of taste and smell by incorporating aphrodisiac foods, flavored lubes, or scented candles into your playtime.

Erogenous Zones in Male and Female Body

Harness the power of sound to enhance arousal and create ambiance. Experiment with erotic music, whispered words of desire, or the sound of each other's breath to heighten anticipation and deepen connection.

Temperature play can also add an exhilarating dimension to sexual experiences. Experiment with warm massage oils, cool breath against the skin, or temperature-controlled toys to awaken the senses and ignite passion.

Exploring Role-Play and Fantasies

Role-play and fantasies offer an opportunity to step into new personas and explore desires beyond the constraints of reality. By tapping into imagination and creativity, partners can infuse their sexual experiences with excitement, novelty, and adventure.

Discuss fantasies and desires openly with your partner, exploring shared interests and boundaries. Create a safe space where both partners feel comfortable expressing their deepest desires and exploring new roles and scenarios.

Experiment with role-play scenarios that cater to your interests and fantasies. Whether it's a naughty nurse and patient, dominant/submissive dynamic, or playful strangers meeting for the first time, allow yourselves to fully immerse in the fantasy and embrace the freedom of expression.

Use props, costumes, and accessories to enhance the role-play experience and bring fantasies to life. From seductive lingerie to role-specific outfits and

Erogenous Zones in Male and Female Body

accessories, let your imagination run wild and indulge in the theatrics of desire.

In integrating erogenous zones into sexual experiences, embrace the full spectrum of sensation, imagination, and connection. Explore the rich tapestry of the human body, engage all the senses, and unleash the power of fantasy to elevate your sexual encounters to new heights of pleasure and intimacy.

Wendy Chad

Chapter 8

Enhancing Intimacy through Erogenous Zone Stimulation

The exploration and stimulation of erogenous zones serve as the gateway to profound connection and heightened pleasure during intimacy. In this chapter, we delve into the ways in which partners can enhance intimacy through shared arousal experiences, using erogenous zone stimulation in foreplay and romantic encounters, and engaging in non-penetrative sexual activities that focus on the exquisite realms of sensation and connection.

Erogenous Zones in Male and Female Body

Building Trust and Emotional Connection through Shared Arousal

Shared arousal experiences create a foundation of trust and emotional intimacy between partners, deepening the bond and strengthening the connection. By exploring each other's erogenous zones with care, curiosity, and enthusiasm, partners can cultivate a sense of safety, vulnerability, and mutual pleasure.

Communication is key in fostering trust and emotional connection. Share desires, boundaries, and fantasies openly with your partner, creating a safe space where both partners feel valued, respected, and heard.

Approach erogenous zone stimulation with attentiveness and empathy, honoring your partner's responses and preferences. Pay attention to verbal and nonverbal cues, and adjust your approach accordingly to ensure mutual enjoyment and comfort.

Express gratitude and appreciation for your partner's willingness to explore and be vulnerable. Celebrate the shared experiences and moments of connection, fostering a sense of closeness and intimacy that transcends the physical realm.

Using Erogenous Zone Stimulation in Foreplay and Romance

Foreplay serves as the prelude to passion, setting the stage for deeper connection and heightened arousal. Incorporating erogenous zone stimulation into foreplay can amplify anticipation, prolong pleasure, and ignite desire.

Erogenous Zones in Male and Female Body

Start by teasing and tantalizing each other's erogenous zones with gentle touches, kisses, and caresses. Experiment with different techniques and sensations to discover what elicits the strongest responses from your partner.

Take your time to explore each other's bodies with reverence and curiosity, savoring the journey of discovery and arousal. Pay attention to your partner's reactions and adjust your approach accordingly to maintain a delicate balance of stimulation and restraint.

Incorporate sensory elements, such as scented candles, soft music, and luxurious fabrics, to create an ambiance of romance and sensuality. Engage all the senses to heighten anticipation and deepen the connection between partners.

Wendy Chad

Engaging in Non-Penetrative Sexual Activities that Focus on Erogenous Zones

Non-penetrative sexual activities offer a wealth of opportunities for exploration and pleasure, focusing on the intricacies of erogenous zone stimulation and connection. From sensual massages to intimate cuddling sessions, these activities allow partners to revel in the delights of touch, intimacy, and shared arousal.

Experiment with sensual massages using aromatic oils and gentle strokes to awaken the senses and relax the body. Focus on erogenous zones such as the back, shoulders, and neck, using varying pressure and techniques to heighten arousal.

Explore intimate cuddling sessions where partners can revel in the warmth and closeness of each other's bodies. Embrace each other tenderly, caressing and

Erogenous Zones in Male and Female Body

exploring erogenous zones with care and affection, deepening the connection and intimacy between partners.

Incorporate playful activities such as blindfolded exploration or sensory deprivation, heightening awareness and sensitivity to touch and sensation. Encourage communication and feedback throughout, allowing partners to guide each other's exploration and pleasure.

In enhancing intimacy through erogenous zone stimulation, embrace the journey of discovery, connection, and pleasure with your partner. Communicate openly, explore with curiosity and reverence, and celebrate the moments of closeness and connection that arise from shared arousal experiences.

Chapter 9

Personalization and Variation

Personalization and variation are the brushstrokes that paint a unique portrait of pleasure and intimacy for each individual. In this chapter, we explore the importance of catering to individual preferences and desires, the journey of discovering new erogenous zones and arousal patterns over time, and the beauty of embracing fluidity in arousal and pleasure responses.

Catering to Individual Preferences and Desires

Every individual is a mosaic of desires, preferences, and boundaries, each as unique as a fingerprint. To truly unlock the depths of pleasure and intimacy,

Erogenous Zones in Male and Female Body

partners must take the time to understand and cater to each other's individual needs and desires.

Communication lies at the heart of personalization, allowing partners to express their desires, boundaries, and fantasies openly and honestly. Take the time to listen attentively to your partner's needs and preferences, and reciprocate with care, respect, and enthusiasm.

Experiment with different techniques, rhythms, and intensities to discover what resonates most with your partner. Pay attention to their verbal and nonverbal cues, and adjust your approach accordingly to ensure mutual enjoyment and satisfaction.

Encourage a spirit of exploration and curiosity, allowing room for discovery and growth as you navigate the ever-evolving landscape of pleasure together. Embrace the opportunity to learn from each other, and celebrate the unique tapestry of desires and preferences that make each sexual encounter a one-of-a-kind experience.

Discovering New Erogenous Zones and Arousal Patterns over Time

The human body is a treasure trove of pleasure, with hidden gems waiting to be discovered and explored. Over time, partners may uncover new erogenous zones and arousal patterns that deepen their connection and expand their repertoire of pleasure.

Approach exploration with an open mind and a spirit of curiosity, allowing yourselves to be surprised and delighted by new discoveries. Pay attention to subtle cues and responses from your partner, and be receptive to the unexpected pleasures that arise along the way.

Erogenous Zones in Male and Female Body

Experiment with different types of touch, pressure, and stimulation to uncover new erogenous zones and arousal patterns. Explore areas of the body that may have been overlooked or underestimated, and allow yourselves to revel in the pleasure of discovery.

Celebrate each new revelation as an opportunity to deepen your intimacy and connection, fostering a sense of wonder and excitement that keeps your sexual experiences fresh and vibrant over time.

Embracing Fluidity in Arousal and Pleasure Responses

Arousal and pleasure are dynamic and fluid experiences, shaped by a myriad of factors including mood, environment, and context. Embracing the fluidity of arousal and pleasure responses allows partners to adapt and respond to each other's needs and desires in the moment.

Recognize that arousal and pleasure can ebb and flow, and that fluctuations are a natural part of the sexual experience. Be patient and compassionate with yourselves and each other, allowing space for spontaneity, exploration, and vulnerability.

Embrace the opportunity to explore different modes of arousal and pleasure, from slow, sensual encounters to more intense and passionate exchanges. Trust in the innate wisdom of your bodies to guide you towards experiences that feel authentic and fulfilling.

Above all, cultivate an atmosphere of acceptance, understanding, and unconditional love, where partners feel free to express themselves fully and authentically. By embracing the fluidity of arousal and pleasure

Erogenous Zones in Male and Female Body

responses, partners can embark on a journey of self-discovery and mutual exploration that enriches their connection and deepens their intimacy over time.

In personalization and variation lies the essence of true intimacy and pleasure. Embrace the uniqueness of each individual, celebrate the diversity of desires and preferences, and revel in the ever-unfolding journey of discovery and connection that awaits you and your partner.

Chapter 10

Beyond the Basics: Advanced Topics and Techniques

In the pursuit of heightened sexuality and improved intimacy, there exists a realm of advanced topics and techniques that delve into the deeper nuances of erogenous zone stimulation. In this chapter, we explore the esoteric realms of tantric and energetic approaches, the exhilarating world of BDSM practices, and the complexities of group play and partner swapping involving erogenous zone stimulation.

Erogenous Zones in Male and Female Body

Tantric and Energetic Approaches to Erogenous Zone Stimulation

Tantric practices offer a profound exploration of sexuality and spirituality, emphasizing the cultivation of energy and connection between partners. Tantric erogenous zone stimulation goes beyond mere physical pleasure, focusing on the exchange of energy and the awakening of dormant sensations within the body.

Incorporate tantric breathing techniques to deepen relaxation and enhance sensitivity to touch. Sync your breath with your partner's, creating a rhythm of connection and intimacy that amplifies arousal and pleasure.

Explore the concept of energetic touch, where the intention behind the touch is as important as the physical sensation itself. Channel your intention and focus into each caress, fostering a sense of presence and connection that transcends the physical realm.

Experiment with tantric rituals such as eye gazing, synchronized movement, and guided meditation to deepen the connection between partners and heighten arousal. Allow yourselves to surrender to the flow of energy and sensation, embracing the transformative power of tantric erogenous zone stimulation.

BDSM Practices and Erogenous Zone Play

BDSM (Bondage, Discipline, Dominance, Submission, Sadism, and Masochism) practices offer a realm of exploration and experimentation for those drawn to the interplay of power dynamics and sensory stimulation. BDSM erogenous zone play encompasses a range of activities aimed at

Erogenous Zones in Male and Female Body

heightening arousal and sensation through the manipulation of power, control, and sensory input.

Explore edging, a practice where arousal is deliberately prolonged through the careful control of stimulation. Tease and tantalize your partner's erogenous zones, bringing them to the brink of orgasm before easing off, building anticipation and intensifying pleasure.

Incorporate sensory deprivation techniques, such as blindfolds or earplugs, to heighten awareness and sensitivity to touch. Depriving one sense can amplify the sensations of others, creating a heightened state of arousal and vulnerability.

Experiment with bondage and restraint, using cuffs, ropes, or other implements to immobilize your partner and enhance their experience of surrender and submission. Trust and communication are paramount in exploring BDSM erogenous zone play, ensuring that all activities are consensual and mutually enjoyable.

Group Play and Partner Swapping Involving Erogenous Zone Stimulation

Group play and partner swapping offer opportunities for exploration and adventure beyond traditional one-on-one encounters. Involving erogenous zone stimulation in group settings adds a layer of complexity and excitement, as multiple partners come together to explore pleasure and connection.

Establish clear communication and boundaries with all parties involved, ensuring that everyone feels comfortable and respected throughout the experience. Discuss desires, expectations, and limits beforehand

Erogenous Zones in Male and Female Body

to create a safe and consensual environment for exploration.

Experiment with different configurations and dynamics, such as threesomes, foursomes, or larger group settings, to explore the possibilities of shared arousal and pleasure. Allow each participant to express their desires and preferences, and prioritize mutual satisfaction and enjoyment.

Embrace the diversity of experiences and connections that arise from group play and partner swapping, recognizing that each encounter offers its own unique opportunities for growth, discovery, and connection. Celebrate the beauty of exploration and experimentation, and honor the trust and intimacy shared among all participants.

Wendy Chad

In exploring advanced topics and techniques in erogenous zone stimulation, embrace the opportunity for growth, discovery, and expansion beyond the confines of conventional sexual practices. Whether delving into the realms of tantra, BDSM, or group play, allow yourselves to explore with curiosity, openness, and a spirit of adventure, unlocking new dimensions of pleasure and intimacy along the way.

Erogenous Zones in Male and Female Body

Wendy Chad

Chapter 11

Enhancing Your Sexual Experience with Erogenous Zone Stimulation

As you journey through the complexities of erogenous zone stimulation, armed with knowledge and curiosity, you embark on a path of profound discovery and heightened pleasure. In this chapter, we delve into the art of incorporating this knowledge into your own sexual experiences, finding new ways to explore and enjoy your partner's and your own erogenous zones, and embracing the power of curiosity and open-mindedness to elevate your sexuality to new heights of fulfillment and intimacy.

Erogenous Zones in Male and Female Body

Putting It All Together: Incorporating Knowledge into Your Sexual Experiences

Integrating the insights gleaned from the previous chapters into your sexual encounters allows you to create a symphony of sensation that resonates deeply with you and your partner. Start by revisiting the fundamental principles of erogenous zone stimulation—communication, consent, and exploration—and apply them with intention and mindfulness.

Communicate openly with your partner about desires, boundaries, and fantasies, creating a safe space where both partners feel empowered to express themselves fully. Draw upon the techniques and practices explored throughout this guide, experimenting with different strokes, pressures, and sensations to tailor your experiences to your unique preferences.

Consider incorporating elements of tantric breathing, sensory play, or BDSM practices into your encounters, allowing yourself to explore new realms of pleasure and connection. Embrace the opportunity for spontaneity and experimentation, trusting in the wisdom of your bodies to guide you towards experiences that feel authentic and fulfilling.

Finding New Ways to Explore and Enjoy Erogenous Zones

As you continue to deepen your understanding of erogenous zones, remain open to discovering new sources of pleasure and arousal within yourself and your partner. Take the time to explore lesser-known areas of the body, such as the inner thighs, neck, ears, and lower back, with curiosity and reverence.

Erogenous Zones in Male and Female Body

Experiment with different types of touch, temperature play, and sensory props to awaken dormant sensations and ignite passion. Encourage your partner to reciprocate, allowing for mutual exploration and discovery that deepens your connection and intimacy.

Incorporate elements of playfulness and creativity into your encounters, embracing the opportunity to experiment with role-play, fantasy, and improvisation. Allow yourselves to let go of inhibitions and expectations, surrendering to the flow of sensation and connection that arises from authentic exploration and expression.

The Power of Curiosity and Open-Mindedness in Enhancing Your Sexuality

Above all, embrace the power of curiosity and open-mindedness as catalysts for growth, discovery, and transformation in your sexual journey. Approach each encounter with a sense of wonder and exploration, remaining open to new experiences and perspectives that expand your understanding of pleasure and intimacy.

Challenge societal norms and expectations surrounding sexuality, embracing your own desires and preferences with confidence and self-assurance. Celebrate the diversity of human sexuality, recognizing that there is no one-size-fits-all approach to pleasure and fulfillment.

Cultivate a mindset of continual learning and growth, seeking out resources, workshops, and communities that support your sexual exploration and development. Surround yourself with like-minded individuals who share your values and aspirations, fostering a sense of belonging and acceptance that empowers you to embrace your sexuality fully.

In enhancing your sexual experience with erogenous zone stimulation, remember that the journey is as important as the destination. Embrace the beauty of exploration, curiosity, and self-discovery, allowing yourself to revel in the boundless possibilities of pleasure and intimacy that await you on this transformative path.

Wendy Chad

Conclusion

Congratulations on completing your journey through the comprehensive exploration guide to erogenous zones in the male and female body! Over the course of this book, you've delved deep into the intricacies of arousal zones, learned techniques for heightened sexuality, and discovered pathways to improved intimacy through erogenous zone stimulation. As you reach the end of this journey, take a moment to reflect on the insights gained and the transformations experienced along the way.

A Journey of Discovery

Throughout this book, you've embarked on a journey of discovery, unraveling the mysteries of the human

Erogenous Zones in Male and Female Body

body and unlocking the secrets of pleasure and intimacy. From the basics of erogenous zone anatomy to advanced techniques in tantric and BDSM practices, you've explored the full spectrum of arousal zones and stimulation techniques with curiosity and enthusiasm.

Empowerment through Knowledge

Armed with knowledge and understanding, you've empowered yourself to take control of your sexual experiences and deepen your connection with your partner. By cultivating communication, consent, and curiosity, you've laid the foundation for fulfilling and mutually satisfying encounters that honor the unique desires and boundaries of both partners.

Wendy Chad

Embracing Diversity and Fluidity

In your exploration of erogenous zones, you've embraced the diversity and fluidity of human sexuality, recognizing that pleasure and intimacy come in many forms. Whether exploring new erogenous zones, experimenting with different techniques, or embracing role-play and fantasy, you've celebrated the richness and complexity of sexual expression.

Continued Growth and Exploration

As you conclude your journey through this guide, remember that the exploration of erogenous zones is a lifelong journey of growth and discovery. Continue to cultivate an open mind and a spirit of curiosity, remaining receptive to new experiences and opportunities for connection and pleasure.

Closing Thoughts

In closing, I encourage you to carry the knowledge and insights gained from this book into your future sexual encounters, approaching each experience with mindfulness, compassion, and a sense of adventure. Whether exploring erogenous zones with a long-term partner or embarking on new adventures with someone new, may you find joy, fulfillment, and connection in every moment of intimacy.

Thank you for joining me on this exploration of erogenous zones in the male and female body. May your journey be filled with pleasure, discovery, and deepened intimacy, and may you continue to embrace the transformative power of erogenous zone stimulation in your life.

Made in the USA
Las Vegas, NV
30 June 2024